Scaredy Kat

Written by Ali Sparkes

Illustrated by Chelen Ecija

1 Fluffy fear

There was so much cooing in the classroom when Katy went in, she wondered if a flock of pigeons had flown in.

There was a crowd around Alina.

"Oooooh!" cooed Lily. "That is soooo cute!"

"Naaaaw!" cooed Alice. "Just want to squeeeeze it!"

"Aaaaah," cooed Tyler. "I *want* one!"

"What is it?" asked Katy.

Alina beamed across at her and said: "You'll never guess!"

"What?" asked Katy.

Alina's brown eyes were shining as she held up a photo. The photo was of a fluffy kitten – a tiny grey tabby with big blue eyes.

3

Katy's smile froze. "Wow!" she whispered,
stepping back. "That's—"

"Adorable!" squeaked Alina, jumping up and down.
"I *know*! Dad brought her home last night.
She's called Pixie."

"Pixie," echoed Katy, as her heartbeat got faster.

"I chose the name," said Alina, grinning from ear
to ear.

"Lovely," said Katy, as her skin prickled.

4

"Can we come and see her?" asked Lily. "She's soooo *gorgeous*!"

"Well, Katy's coming first," said Alina, "because she's my best friend. But you can all come afterwards. Katy ... Katy ...?"

From the school corridor, Katy heard Alina calling, wondering where her best friend had gone.

Because Katy had just run away.

2 Panic pocket

"Katy Carpenter – why are you in the corridor?"

Katy jumped. Mr Driscoll, the head teacher, was standing behind her, his arms folded across his Puggle School T-shirt. One of his shaggy brown eyebrows was up.

"Sorry, Mr Driscoll. I was … just going – " Katy looked around, "– to get something from my coat pocket."

Mr Driscoll glanced along towards the coats and gave a little snort. "Very well, Katy," he said, stepping backwards. "But be quick. You should be in class."

"Yes, sir," said Katy, and ran to her coat. Mr Driscoll had backed away along the corridor, but he was still watching her and she could tell that his eyebrow was still up.

Her coat smelt of home … nice and safe. Katy suddenly remembered there *was* something in her pocket that she needed – a tiny old-fashioned purse, covered in glittery gold beads with a big pearly button. It had belonged to her great-grandmother. Mum said Great-Granny had taken it to dances when she was a girl.

Katy walked quickly back to class, where Mr Driscoll was talking to her teacher, Miss Peebles.

Katy waved the purse. "It's for show and tell, sir!" she said.

"Ooh, that's lovely," said Miss Peebles, taking it. It twinkled as she turned it over.

Mr Driscoll made that strange snorting noise again, turned and walked away.

Katy was relieved to see Alina sitting at her table with a book. The others had gone to their seats too, and nobody was going on about the … about … Alina's new pet.

But as soon as Katy sat down next to her, Alina whispered: "Come and see Pixie on the way home today."

"Um – " Katy whispered back. "I can't. Mum said I have to go straight home."

"What for?" asked Alina, looking disappointed.

"I … I think we have to go out somewhere," said Katy.

Alina looked a bit hurt, but then the lesson started and she had to stop talking about Pixie.

Even so, Katy couldn't stop *thinking* about Pixie. And every time she did, she felt sick.

3 Worrying walk

After school, Lily, Alice and Tyler went home with Alina to meet the new kitten.

Katy felt bad. *She* was Alina's best friend and was supposed to meet Pixie first – but she knew it was her own fault.

She'd suddenly absolutely *had* to sort out her drawer. All her workbooks needed to be put in the right order.

After that, it was vital that she walked across the playground *very slowly*.

And by the time she reached the gate, Alina and the others had gone.

"Everything all right, Katy?"

Katy jumped. It was Mr Driscoll.

"Yes," she squeaked. Mr Driscoll peered at her. "I'm fine," she added, nibbling anxiously on one of the big buttons on her coat.

Mr Driscoll made that odd snorty noise again and quickly went back into school.

Katy went home … but just as she was walking quickly past Alina's house, her friend came running out, holding something fluffy.

"Katy! Just have a quick look!" she called, as Alice, Lily and Tyler watched behind her.

"I can't!" yelled Katy. She began to run.

"Katy!" yelled Alina.

Katy didn't dare to turn back, even though she could hear Alice saying: "What's all *that* about? I thought she was your best friend, Alina!"

Katy ran all the way and arrived home puffing and panting and ... very slightly crying.

"What's wrong?" asked Mum, as soon as she saw her.

"Alina's got a new kitten!" sobbed Katy.

"Aaah," said Mum. "I see."

4 Fearful feelings

How can anyone be scared of a kitten?

Katy had asked herself this so many times. People were scared of spiders. People were scared of snakes … but every person she knew thought that nothing could be cuter than a little fluffy kitten.

If Katy ever saw a kitten or a cat or even a *picture* of a kitten or a cat, her whole body would shake. Her insides would crunch up. Her skin would get covered in goose bumps.

If she saw a cat in the street, she would cross the road to get away from it.

"It's not your fault," said Mum, as they sat at the kitchen table. "Tell Alina about it. She'll understand. I'll take you round to her house now if you like."

"But … I can't go *in* there!" said Katy. "I can't go in Alina's house ever again –"

"But – " said Mum.

"No!" Katy stood up. "I can't. I will *never* be able to go to her house. She'll have to get a new best friend."

"But – " said Mum.

"Everyone will laugh if they find out," said Katy. "I can't tell them. I just can't."

5 Nervous no-mates

Next morning in school was awful. Alina didn't talk about Pixie. She didn't ask Katy why she'd run away. She didn't say anything at all. She had gone to sit with Lily.

Katy sat down at her table with a sad bump.

At breaktime, she walked around the playground alone, while Alina played games with Lily, Alice and Tyler. Katy felt lonely and stupid. Could this day get any worse?

It got worse.

"Children," said Miss Peebles. "We're very lucky! Alina's mum has brought in someone for you all to meet."

Katy froze in her seat. This couldn't be happening! Mrs Patel carried in a small basket with a little wire gate in the front. Behind it ... mewing and squeaking ... was PIXIE!

The whole class erupted.

"Sit down everyone – don't frighten the kitten!" said Miss Peebles.

Don't frighten *the kitten*? The only frightened thing in the room was Katy. Her heartbeat was thundering in her head.

Now Mrs Patel was undoing the little gate. Now she was taking the kitten out … Now she was holding it up for everyone to see … and now she was bringing it across to Katy!

Katy shrieked, kicked over her chair and ran away.

6 Terrifying truths

She screamed all the way down the corridor.

Mr Driscoll sprang out of his office and called: "Katy! What's wrong?"

She kept running, terrified that the kitten was chasing down the corridor after her. She didn't dare look back.

"Katy! Stop! Tell me what's wrong!" yelled Mr Driscoll.

Katy hurtled into the coat pegs area and buried her face in her coat. She expected Mr Driscoll to arrive right behind her and demand to know what was going on.

But he didn't. After a few seconds, Katy pulled her face out of her hood and looked around. Mr Driscoll was standing quite still in the middle of the coat pegs area. He wasn't looking at her at all. He was staring at Tyler's coat.

It lay on the floor … just an ordinary coat, with a hood and big blue buttons down the front.

Katy stopped crying and walked across to the coat. Mr Driscoll was making that snorting sound again. She picked up the coat, and Mr Driscoll gave a little squeak and backed away.

"Um … Katy –" he croaked. "Are you all right? What's going on?"

"I … I'm scared," admitted Katy.

Mr Driscoll gulped. "I'll tell you something, Katy," he said. "I'm scared too."

"But I'm so stupid," said Katy, shakily hanging up Tyler's coat. "I'm scared of kittens! Have you ever heard of anything so stupid?"

"Well – " said Mr Driscoll. "I *might* have heard of something more stupid. You see … *I'm* scared of buttons."

7 Cocoa and confessions

"I was only three," said Katy. She took a sip of
her hot chocolate. Miss Peebles had brought some
for her and for Mr Driscoll as they both sat in
the quiet reception area.

"I was only four," said Mr Driscoll. "What happened
to you?"

"I was out in my buggy," said Katy. "A cat jumped
off the wall and into my buggy and scratched
my face – here." She pointed to her cheek.
"See! There's still a tiny scar."

Mr Driscoll peered at her cheek. "Ah yes," he said.
"I can just about see it."

"Ever since then, I've been scared of cats," said Katy.
"I can't help it. Everyone says they can't really
hurt me, but it doesn't make any difference. I'm just
so scared of them."

Mr Driscoll nodded. "I know what you mean," he said.

"What happened when you were four?" asked Katy, trying to imagine what Mr Driscoll could have looked like at four years old.

"I was playing in my sister's room," said Mr Driscoll. "I found a button on the floor and put it in my mouth. It got stuck in my throat. My dad had to hang me upside down and bash my back to get it out again. Ever since then, I've been terrified of buttons. I know it doesn't make sense ... but I can't seem to help it."

29

"But … people wear buttons all the time!" said Katy.

"Not in this school," said Mr Driscoll. "Everyone here wears T-shirts or jumpers. Haven't you noticed? I made sure of it. No shirts or cardigans … no buttons."

Katy suddenly realised that even the teachers wore Puggle School T-shirts and jumpers.

"The only problem," said Mr Driscoll, with a shiver, "is all the coats. I can make it a rule that everyone has to wear T-shirts and jumpers without buttons – but I can't stop everyone wearing coats with buttons on, can I? So I don't go into the coat pegs area. It's just too scary."

"So … what are we going to do?" asked Katy. "All our lives we're going to meet kittens and buttons!"

"I think I might have a plan," said Mr Driscoll.

31

8 Breathe and be brave

Two days later, a speaker called Frances came into assembly to talk about phobias.

"Phobias are fears," she explained. "We all have fears. We're scared of falling off cliffs or getting bitten by sharks. These are normal fears. But when we get scared of an everyday thing that can't really hurt us, and when that fear gets so big it stops us having a normal, happy life – that's a phobia."

Then she asked everyone what they were scared of.

Lily flung up her hand. "Spiders!"

A few of the others said spiders too. Some said snakes. Mr Jackson said he was a bit scared of water. "I'm not a good swimmer," he admitted. Miss Peebles said she was so scared of heights that she couldn't even go up a ladder.

"Has anyone got any
unusual phobias?" asked Frances.

Katy felt her heart speed up.
Mr Driscoll nodded at her. She put up
her hand.

"Yes?" said Frances.

"I – " Katy gulped. "I'm scared of – "
She gulped again and looked
at Alina. "Kittens."

Everyone gasped – but before there was
time for anyone to laugh, Mr Driscoll
called out: "And I'm scared of buttons."

And *then* everyone laughed.
Until Frances held up her hands
and said: "Wait … these are very
unusual phobias. Do you know *why*
you're afraid of them?"

"Katy," said Mr Driscoll, "come up
to the front with me. If you can tell
your story, I'll tell mine."

35

Five minutes later, everyone was staring at them, open-mouthed. Katy had told her story and Mr Driscoll had told his. There was a long silence. Katy could hardly breathe. Everyone would laugh at her about this *forever* … and probably at Mr Driscoll too.

Then Alina stood up. "Katy! You should have *told* me!"

"I know," said Katy.

"You might be scared of kittens," Alina went on, "but you're the bravest person I know for standing up and telling everyone. Except maybe Mr Driscoll."

And then everyone started clapping.

39

9 Calm, calm, calm …

It turned out that the only way for Katy and
Mr Driscoll to get over their phobias was to face
them … a little bit at a time.

1. Katy had to keep looking at a picture of
    Pixie until her heartbeat settled down.

2. Mr Driscoll had to look at a picture of a
    button until *his* heartbeat settled down.

3. Katy had to hold Pixie's collar for five minutes.

4. Mr Driscoll had to sit in the coat pegs area for half an hour.

5. Katy had to go around to Alina's house and watch while Alina held Pixie.

6. Mr Driscoll had to touch a coat with buttons on it.

7. Katy had to stand a bit closer to the kitten and wait for her heart to slow down again.

8. Mr Driscoll had to touch a button.

9. Katy had to put her finger on Pixie's head.

10. Mr Driscoll had to hold a button.

It took three weeks and then, one day, Katy could actually *pick Pixie up*!

And Mr Driscoll could actually *wear* a shirt with buttons on it.

When they went back into assembly with Mr Driscoll in his shirt with buttons and Katy holding Pixie, the whole school cheered.

And laughed.

But in a nice way …

THE PUGGLE

PHOBIA WORKSHOPS LAUNCHED AT PUGGLE SCHOOL

THE CHILDREN OF PUGGLE are running workshops at their school this week – to help people with phobias.

Head teacher Mr Peter Driscoll, 39, and eight-year-old pupil Katy Carpenter launched the workshop week with a talk about overcoming their unusual phobias.

"I've had a massive fear of buttons since I nearly choked on one when I was four," said Mr Driscoll.

BUGLE

"After Katy told me she had a phobia of kittens, we decided to get help. Now we're so much better and we want to help others."

"I was so scared of my friend's kitten," said Katy. "But now I can hold Pixie and I love her!"

Dozens of Puggle people have signed up for the workshops, with phobias including: spiders, snakes, heights, hair, clowns and ... mashed potato.

Ideas for reading

Written by Christine Whitney
Primary Literacy Consultant

Reading objectives:
- discuss the sequence of events in books
- make inferences on the basis of what is being said and done
- answer and ask questions
- predict what might happen on the basis of what has been read so far

Spoken language objectives:
- ask relevant questions to extend their understanding and knowledge
- use spoken language to develop understanding through speculating, hypothesising, imagining and exploring ideas
- participate in discussions, presentations, role play, improvisations and debates

Curriculum links: PSHE – relationships, health and well-being

Word count: 2491

Interest words: anxiously, phobias, open-mouthed

Resources: exercise books and pencils

Build a context for reading

- Ask children if they have heard of the phrase "scaredy cat" before. Do they know what it means?

- Look at the image on the front cover and title. Ask children to explain what the author has done with the title *Scaredy Kat*.

- Read the blurb together. Look again at the front cover and discuss what they think Katy is afraid of and who else might have a phobia. Discuss the meaning of the word *phobias*.

Understand and apply reading strategies

- Read the title to Chapter 1. Ask children what they think might happen. Help them to notice that the author created a title for each chapter that uses alliteration. Ask children to jot down the titles to the chapters as they read on through the book and to note the alliteration.